MAKING IT HAPPEN

By EMILY ARROW

Illustrations by NOÉMIE GIONET LANDRY

Music by EMILY ARROW

CANTATA
LEARNING

WWW.CANTATALEARNING.COM

CANTATA LEARNING

Published by Cantata Learning
1710 Roe Crest Drive
North Mankato, MN 56003
www.cantatalearning.com

Library of Congress Cataloging-in-Publication Data

Names: Arrow, Emily, author. | Landry, Noémie Gionet, illustrator.
Title: Making it happen / by Emily Arrow ; illustrated by Noémie Gionet
  Landry ; music by Emily Arrow.
Description: North Mankato, MN : Cantata Learning, [2020] | Series: My
  feelings, my choices | Includes bibliographical references.
Identifiers: LCCN 2018053379 (print) | LCCN 2018055661 (ebook) | ISBN
  9781684104208 (eBook) | ISBN 9781684104055 (hardcover) | ISBN
  9781684104321 (pbk.)
Subjects: LCSH: Goal (Psychology)--Juvenile literature. | Motivation
  (Psychology) in children--Juvenile literature.
Classification: LCC BF505.G6 (ebook) | LCC BF505.G6 A77 2020 (print) | DDC
  158.1--dc23
LC record available at https://lccn.loc.gov/2018053379

Book design and art direction: Tim Palin Creative
Editorial direction: Kellie M. Hultgren
Music direction: Elizabeth Draper
Music composed and produced by Emily Arrow

Printed in the United States of America.
0406

ACCESS THE MUSIC!

SCAN CODE WITH MOBILE APP

CANTATALEARNING.COM

TIPS TO SUPPORT LITERACY AT HOME

WHY READING AND SINGING WITH YOUR CHILD IS SO IMPORTANT

Daily reading with your child leads to increased academic achievement. Music and songs, specifically rhyming songs, are a fun and easy way to build early literacy and language development. Music skills correlate significantly with both phonological awareness and reading development. Singing helps build vocabulary and speech development. And reading and appreciating music together is a wonderful way to strengthen your relationship.

READ AND SING EVERY DAY!

TIPS FOR USING CANTATA LEARNING BOOKS AND SONGS DURING YOUR DAILY STORY TIME

1. As you sing and read, point out the different words on the page that rhyme. Suggest other words that rhyme.

2. Memorize simple rhymes such as Itsy Bitsy Spider and sing them together. This encourages comprehension skills and early literacy skills.

3. Use the questions in the back of each book to guide your singing and storytelling.

4. Read the included sheet music with your child while you listen to the song. How do the music notes correlate to the words of the song?

5. Sing along on the go and at home. Access music by scanning the QR code on each Cantata book. You can also stream or download the music for free to your computer, smartphone, or mobile device.

Devoting time to daily reading shows that you are available for your child. Together, you are building language, literacy, and listening skills.

Have fun reading and singing!

Have you ever felt **proud** of something you did or learned? Maybe you wrote a story or learned to do a cartwheel. What are some other things you want to do? Would you like to learn to read a whole book on your own? Maybe you want to learn to play an instrument. These are examples of **goals**. A goal is a thing you want to do. For each goal you have, there are **steps** you can take to make it happen.

Are you ready to make it happen? Turn the page and sing along!

Kite festival
(Next Saturday)

G-O-A-L Goal! It's something you want to do,
like try something new.

G-O-A-L Goal! Let's make a goal
to build and fly a kite.

What's the goal? To build and fly a kite.

When do you want to reach your goal?

Make a **plan**!

What are the steps to reach your goal? Now begin!

Get a little bit closer every day,

and when you reach your goal, shout, "Hooray!

Hooray! Hooray, hey, hey, hey!"

Oh, you're making it happen.

Oh, you're making it happen.

G-O-A-L Goal! Goals can be tiny or big,
like a dream or a wish.

G-O-A-L Goal! What do you need
to try to build a kite?

Get supplies to try to build a kite.

When do you want to reach your goal?

Make a plan!

What are the steps to reach your goal? Now begin!

Get a little bit closer every day,

and when you reach your goal, shout, "Hooray!

Hooray! Hooray, hey, hey, hey!"

Oh, you're making it happen.

Oh, you're making it happen.

Steps
1) Find materials
2) Tie the frame
3) Attach sail to frame
4) Attach flying string
5) Tie ribbon balance

DIAMOND KITE
Materials

Box Kite
How to assemble:

DELTA KITE

13

You might try to reach a goal, try to reach a goal, but it might not happen like you planned.

So if you try to reach a goal, try to reach a goal, just remember that a goal is changeable.

When do you want to reach your goal?

Make a plan!

What are the steps to reach your goal? Now begin!

Get a little bit closer every day,

and when you reach your goal, shout, "Hooray!

Hooray! Hooray, hey, hey, hey!"

Oh, you're making it happen.

Oh, you're making it happen.

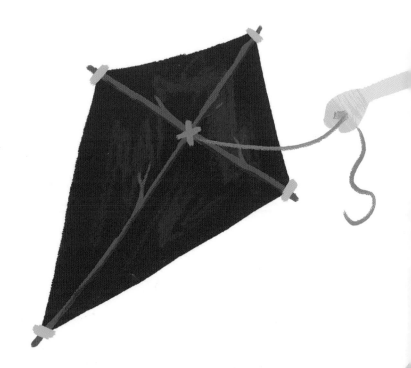

Steps
1) Find materials
2) Tie the frame
3) Attach sail to frame
4) Attach string
5) Tie ribbon balance

DIAMOND KITE
Materials

G-O-A-L Goal! Goals can take a long, long time, but we keep on trying.

G-O-A-L Goal! You're getting close. It's almost time to fly.

Get your kite! It's almost time to fly!

KITE
FESTIVAL
POSTPONED
(TOMORROW)

19

Oh, you're making it happen.
Oh, you're making it happen.

Step by step, the closer you get.
You are making it happen!
You are making it happen!

SONG LYRICS
Making It Happen

G-O-A-L Goal! It's something you want to do,
like try something new.
G-O-A-L Goal! Let's make a goal
to build and fly a kite.
What's the goal? To build and fly a kite.

When do you want to reach your goal? Make a plan!
What are the steps to reach your goal? Now begin!
Get a little bit closer every day,
and when you reach your goal, shout, "Hooray!
Hooray! Hooray, hey, hey, hey!"
Oh, you're making it happen.
Oh, you're making it happen.

G-O-A-L Goal! Goals can be tiny or big,
like a dream or a wish.
G-O-A-L Goal! What do you need
to try to build a kite?
Get supplies to try to build a kite.

When do you want to reach your goal? Make a plan!
What are the steps to reach your goal? Now begin!
Get a little bit closer every day,
and when you reach your goal, shout, "Hooray!
Hooray! Hooray, hey, hey, hey!"
Oh, you're making it happen.
Oh, you're making it happen.

You might try to reach a goal, try to reach a goal,
but it might not happen like you planned.
So if you try to reach a goal, try to reach a goal,
just remember that a goal is changeable.

When do you want to reach your goal? Make a plan!
What are the steps to reach your goal? Now begin!
Get a little bit closer every day,
and when you reach your goal, shout, "Hooray!
Hooray! Hooray, hey, hey, hey!"
Oh, you're making it happen.
Oh, you're making it happen.

G-O-A-L Goal! Goals can take a long, long time,
but we keep on trying.
G-O-A-L Goal! You're getting close.
It's almost time to fly.
Get your kite! It's almost time to fly!

Oh, you're making it happen.
Oh, you're making it happen.
Step by step, the closer you get.
You are making it happen!
You are making it happen!

Making It Happen

Kindie
Emily Arrow

Verse

1. G - O - A - L Goal! It's some-thing you want to do, like try some-thing new. G - O - A - L Goal! Let's make a goal to build and
fly a kite. What's the goal? To build and fly a kite.

Chorus

When do you want to reach your goal? Make a plan! What are the steps to reach your goal? Now be-gin! Get a lit-tle bit clos-er eve-ry day, and when you reach your goal, shout, "Hooray! Hoo-ray! Hoo-ray, hey, hey, hey!" Oh, you're mak-ing it hap-pen. Oh, you're mak-ing it hap-pen.

Verse 2
G-O-A-L Goal! Goals can be tiny or big,
like a dream or a wish.
G-O-A-L Goal! What do you need
to try to build a kite?
Get supplies to try to build a kite.

Chorus

Bridge

You might try to reach a goal, try to reach a goal, but it might not hap-pen like you planned. So if you try to reach a goal,
try to reach a goal, just re-mem-ber that a goal is change-a-ble.

Chorus

Verse 3
G-O-A-L Goal! Goals can take a long, long time,
but we keep on trying.
G-O-A-L Goal! You're getting close.
It's almost time to fly.
Get your kite! It's almost time to fly!

Outro

Oh, you're mak-ing it hap-pen. Oh, you're mak-ing it hap-pen. Step by step, the clos-er you get. You are mak-ing it hap-pen!
You are mak-ing it hap-pen!

23

GLOSSARY

goals—things you want to do

plan—the steps you need to take to reach a goal

proud—happy about yourself for something you've done

steps—things you have to do to reach a goal

CRITICAL THINKING QUESTIONS

1. Have you ever made a goal for yourself? What was the first step you took toward that goal? What steps did you take after that? Draw pictures of three steps you took.

2. Tell about a time when someone you know decided on a goal and then made it happen. How do you think that person felt after reaching the goal? Did you celebrate together?

3. Sometimes you might want to change your goal. Tell about a time when you had a goal and then changed your mind. What new goal did you pick?

TO LEARN MORE

Barnett, Mac. *Sam and Dave Dig a Hole*. Somerville, MA: Candlewick, 2014.

Hoena, Blake. *These Are the Chores We Do*. North Mankato, MN: Cantata Learning, 2016.

Reynolds, Peter. *Sky Color*. Somerville, MA: Candlewick, 2012.

Yamada, Kobi. *What Do You Do with an Idea?* Seattle, WA: Compendium, 2014.